The Race of Toad and Deer

The Race of
Toad and Deer

RETOLD BY PAT MORA
ILLUSTRATED BY MAYA ITZNA BROOKS

ORCHARD BOOKS • NEW YORK

For Teresa McKenna and Tey Diana Rebolledo,
my friends in the race
—P.M.

To my mother, Nan, for bringing me into the art world,
and my husband, Maury, for his advice and inspiration
— M.I.B.

Note: The author heard this folktale from Don Fernando Tesucún, a mason of restoration at the Guatemalan archaeological site of Tikál. Don Fernando, who actively documents his native language of Itzaj Maya, often guides visiting scholars through the jungles and pyramids of Tikál.

Text copyright © 1995 by Pat Mora
Illustrations copyright © 1995 by Maya Itzna Brooks

Orchard Books, 95 Madison Avenue, New York, NY 10016

Manufactured in the United States of America. Printed by Barton Press, Inc.
Bound by Horowitz/Rae. Book design by Susan Phillips.

The text of this book is set in 12 point Stone Sans Bold.
The illustrations are gouache and casein reproduced in full color.
10 9 8 7 6 5 4 3 2 1

Library of Congress Cataloging-in-Publication Data
Mora, Pat. The race of toad and deer / retold by Pat Mora; illustrated by Maya Itzna Brooks.
p. cm. Summary: With the help of his friends, Tio Sapo, the toad, defeats the overconfident
Tio Venado, the deer, in a race.
ISBN 0-531-09477-4. –ISBN 0-531-08777-8 (lib. bdg.) [1. Folklore–Guatemala.] I. Brooks,
Maya Itzna, ill. II. Title. PZ8.1.M795Rac 1995 398.2 ' 097281 ' 045787–dc20 [E] 94-45919

The moon rose slowly over the jungle. Sapo and his friends were singing and singing at their favorite pond.

They sang so loudly they did not hear the large creature moving toward them.

"*Silencio*. Stop all this racket," growled Venado, the largest deer in the jungle. "I want quiet when I drink."

The toads were angry and frightened. But Sapo just went on singing.

"I said quiet!" snarled Venado. "I am the ruler of this jungle. I am the biggest and the fastest."

"Not faster than I am," squeaked Sapo,
stretching as tall and sounding as brave as he could.
Venado laughed. "Uncle Toad, dear Tío Sapo,
I'll race you tomorrow, and we'll see who wins."

As the sun rose over the green jungle, parrots squawked the news. "Race today! *¡Carrera hoy!* Race today!"

"Who's racing?" asked the spider monkeys swinging through the trees. "Who's racing?"

In the shade, Jaguar yawned. "Toad and Deer will race today."

"Yes, Sapo and Venado will race today!" chattered the spider monkeys.

The parrots and monkeys
hid in the trees and watched
Venado look at himself in a lake.
He lifted his proud head. "I am
the fastest runner in the jungle,"
said the deer to himself. "My legs
are swifter than the wind.
I always win."
At the other end of the lake, Sapo wished
his friends a good morning. Bowing slightly,
he said, "*Buenos días, mis amigos.*"
"*Buenos días, Sapo,*" answered his friends.
"We know you can win the race, Sapo. You can!"
they shouted, hopping up and down in excitement.

"I can win only if you help me," said Sapo. "*Mis amigos,* will you help me win the race today?"

"We are your *amigos*, Sapo," croaked an old toad very slowly. "Of course we will help you win. You are a smart one, and you always have a plan. What must we do?"

"Come close and I'll tell you," whispered Sapo.

Late that afternoon as the sun was setting, parrots called out, "Race time! ¡Carrera! ¡Carrera!"

All the animals of the jungle came. Toucans and butterflies rushed through the trees. Spider monkeys swung from limb to limb. Armadillos, javelinas, anteaters, iguanas, and bush dogs moved through the steamy jungle, all eager to watch the race.

Soon tapirs, big-eyed crocodiles, pheasants, and wild turkeys lined the dirt path. They shouted, *"Buenas tardes, buenas tardes,"* to the jaguars stretched out in shady branches to watch from above. In the leaves and roots along the path, Sapo's friends were hiding, ready to help their friend.

"Ready, Tío Sapo?" asked Venado, kicking a bit of dirt, puffing his chest, and looking down at Sapo.
"Ready, Uncle Deer!" shouted Sapo, wiping the dirt from his eyes and stretching as tall as he could.
Old Toucan yelled, "GO!"

Down the path raced Sapo and Venado. After a few leaps, Venado called back, as he always did, "*Adelante*, Tío Sapo, forward!"

To Venado's surprise, from down the path he heard a toad voice shout, "*Adelante*, Tío Venado, forward!"

Venado was confused. He raced faster.

Sapo hopped steadily, steadily down the path,
but Venado raced faster and faster. His legs began to
hurt, but he kept leaping farther and farther. He was
becoming tired, very tired. One last time he gasped,
"*Adelante*, Tío Sapo."

Again, "*¡Adelante*, Tío Venado!" He heard a toad's
voice down the path.

Finally, Venado saw the finish line. Venado's strong legs were shaking. His tongue was hanging out. He was panting so hard from racing faster and leaping farther that he could barely move.

But Sapo just hopped steadily, steadily down the path as voices shouted, "Go, Sapo, go!"

Yes, Sapo hopped right by tired, proud Venado gasping for breath. When he neared the finish line, Sapo called back, "¡Adelante, Tío Venado!"

"Sapo won! Sapo won!" shouted the jungle animals.

Sapo bowed slightly to all his friends. He said, "*WE* won the race, *mis amigos!* Together, we won the big race!"

Toucan called Venado forward to place the
crown on Sapo's small head. Venado shuffled forward
very slowly, in no hurry. Suddenly, he heard many toad
voices shouting, calling him forward. *"¡Adelante, Tío
Venado!"*